DATE DUE			
APR 2 6 '01			
MAY 1 7 01			

2/01

HEADQUARTERS
413 West Main Street
Medford, Oregon 97501

MARVIN
and the
Meanest Girl

Suzy Kline

MARVIN
and the
Meanest Girl

Illustrated by Blanche Sims

G. P. PUTNAM'S SONS   NEW YORK

Many thanks to Anne O'Connell for her
valuable help with this book.

Text copyright © 2000 by Suzy Kline
Illustrations copyright © 2000 by Blanche Sims
All rights reserved. This book, or parts thereof, may not be
reproduced in any form without permission in writing from the
publisher. G. P. Putnam's Sons, a division of Penguin Putnam Books
for Young Readers, 345 Hudson Street, New York, NY 10014.
G. P. Putnam's Sons, Reg. U.S. Pat. & Tm. Off.
Published simultaneously in Canada. Printed in the United States of America.
Designed by Marikka Tamura and Gina DiMassi. Text set in Sabon.
Library of Congress Cataloging-in-Publication Data
Kline, Suzy. Marvin and the meanest girl / Suzy Kline; illustrated by
Blanche Sims. p. cm. SUMMARY: Marvin thinks that the new girl in class,
Lucy Tinker, is a liar and a thief, but then he finds that he may have misjudged
her. [1. Schools—Fiction. 2. Friendship—Fiction.] I. Sims, Blanche, ill.
II. Title. PZ27.K6797 Mal 2000 [Fic]—dc21 99-20925 CIP
ISBN 0-399-23409-8
1   3   5   7   9   10   8   6   4   2
First Impression

Dedicated with love to my mother,
Martha S. Weaver. Thank you for
being my forever friend.
—S. K.

Contents

1

The Meanest Girl

Marvin copied five numbers in his journal from his little yellow notebook:

984; 85; 3; 63; 1,000,000

Audrey leaned over and asked, "What are you doing? We're supposed to be writing a story."

"These five numbers tell a story."

"Pa . . . leeesse," Audrey replied. "A story is supposed to have a beginning, middle, and ending. Your story is just a list of numbers."

Marvin watched Audrey turn and whisper something to her best friend, Elizabeth. When they giggled, Marvin thought, Wait till I read my story aloud. I'll show them!

Then he looked over at the new girl in their room, Lucy Tinker. Her short hair stuck out like porcupine quills.

"Hey, porcupine!" he called.

Lucy ignored him. She was busy

making something out of clay. Her hands were halfway inside her desk so the teacher couldn't see. Marvin wondered why Audrey didn't bug *Lucy* about not writing.

"Hey, Tinker, you're a stinker!" he joked.

Lucy turned abruptly and stuck out her tongue. Then she returned to her clay-making.

Marvin laughed as he kept spying on her.

He noticed a wooden box that was tucked inside her desk. It was the old-fashioned kind that once had cigars in it. He wondered if there was still a cigar in there.

As Marvin watched Lucy shape the green clay in her desk, he noticed something else.

Her fingernails.

Each one was polished a different color. The thumbnail was red, the pointer finger was yellow, the middle finger was sky blue, the ring finger was green, and the little finger was pink.

Marvin leaned over and whispered, "I think your fingernail polish looks *dumb*."

Lucy turned to face Marvin again, only this time she lowered her eyelids slowly like shades on windows. As soon as her eyes were barely blue slits, she leaned over and scratched his arm.

"Hey!" Marvin jerked back. He stared at the two white lines etched in his skin. They reminded him of the skate marks he had made on the ice during winter.

Mrs. Bird stopped writing in her

notebook and looked up. "Is there a problem?" she asked.

Marvin shook his head. He was no tattletale. Right now, he was trying to rub the white marks away with his hand, but they wouldn't disappear.

When writing time was finished, Mrs. Bird asked, "Who would like to share the story they wrote this morning?"

Marvin forgot his pain and waved his hand.

"Okay, you go first, Marvin," the teacher said. "Does your story have a title?"

Marvin cleared his throat proudly. He always titled his numbers. "Yes. The Eiffel Tower."

When Audrey rolled her eyes and Elizabeth giggled, Marvin thought, I'll show them now.

He held his journal carefully so only he could see the numbers:

The Eiffel Tower
984; 85; 3; 63; 1,000,000.

"The Eiffel Tower is nine hundred eighty-four feet high. On a clear day, you can see eighty-five miles from the top. It has three elevators. Each elevator can carry sixty-three people. It cost about one million dollars to build the Eiffel Tower."

"Amazing!" Mrs. Bird exclaimed.

"How did you know so many facts about the Eiffel Tower?"

Marvin closed his writing journal. "From different websites on my computer," he answered. "I collect interesting *statistics.*" He liked using that S word. That's what his dad said he did for a job. Worked with statistics.

Thinking about S words, Marvin looked back at the *new girl,* Miss Scratcho! She was making a green snake out of clay. Each time she rubbed it between her hands, the snake got longer and longer.

When Lucy noticed that Marvin was staring at her, she held up the snake and made it talk. "Hsssssssss!" she hissed. "You said I was a porcupine. Well, you're a snake! A *poisonous* one!"

Now Marvin shook his head. She always had to get even, he thought. "You're the *meanest* girl I know," he snapped.

Lucy just *hisssssssed* some more.

Marvin whipped out his notebook and titled a fresh page.

Lucy Porcupine Tinker Stinker
5, 5, 1

Silently, he read his short story to himself:

Lucy has five dumb colors on her five fingernails, and she scratched me once. I will bug her back. I just have to figure out how and when.

2

The Golden Game

The next morning, Marvin and Fred walked into the science corner of their classroom.

"I like being science monitor, don't you?" Fred asked.

"Yeah," Marvin replied, half listening. He was trying to think of a little game to play on Lucy Tinker.

"I'll feed Cuddles," Fred said, giving the guinea pig some small carrots and lettuce. "You feed the tropical fish. Their can of food is supposed to be next to the tank, but someone didn't put it back right."

"Okay," Marvin said as he squatted down and started searching for the small yellow container in the cupboard below. After he rooted around awhile, he found it in a bucket of pattern blocks. Someone had put it in the wrong place. What a *pain!* he thought.

Suddenly, Marvin stood up.

What if something that belonged to Lucy turned up in the wrong place?

Would that bother her?

Yeeeeeees!

Marvin grinned from ear to ear. He had his little game!

Marvin glanced over at Lucy. She was sitting at her desk fiddling with green clay again.

"Unless you're doing a monitor chore," Mrs. Bird announced, "you should be working on the math problems I put on the board."

Lucy raised one finger to go to the bathroom.

After Mrs. Bird nodded, Lucy left the room.

Marvin followed her to the doorway and watched her leave. On the way, she stopped and opened up her red bookbag, took out a comb with a pearl handle, and then skipped down the hall.

Marvin hurried back into the room and over to her desk. Everyone was working on math problems except for Fred, who was feeding Cuddles, Mary Marony, who was dusting the library bookshelf, and Audrey, who was watering the bean plants.

Mrs. Bird was looking for something on her desk.

It was safe!

Marvin kneeled down and looked inside Lucy's desk. It was messy and stuffed with wadded-up paper and chunks of clay. The only thing that looked interesting was the wooden cigar box.

Marvin pulled it out and opened the lid. No cigars.

But, there was *something* interesting inside it.

A rock about the size of a golf ball. It was pure gold! The sides were chiseled and jagged and sparkled in the sunlight from the window.

Wow! Marvin thought. It felt cold and heavy in his hand. Carefully, he placed the gold rock back between a purple pencil with a volleyball eraser

and a pink pencil with a clown eraser.

He closed the box and stepped out-side the classroom. There was still time. The final bell hadn't rung yet. He spot-ted Lucy's red bookbag. It was still unbuckled. He put the cigar box inside and smiled. When he returned to the science corner, he joined Fred.

"Look at Cuddles gnaw this carrot," Fred said. "She eats it right out of my hand. Did you find the fish food okay?"

"Yup," Marvin replied, sprinkling some flakes in the tank.

"All plants watered!" Audrey said as she checked off Tuesday on the bean chart.

Mary Marony hung up the duster by the bookshelves.

Shortly after the monitors returned to their seats, the bell rang and the class said the pledge.

Marvin put his hand over his heart, but he didn't say the pledge. He was too busy picturing what was going to happen. Lucy would walk up the stairs, return the comb to her red bookbag, and find the cigar box. Her jaw would drop. Her eyes would bug out! And she'd say, HOW DID MY CIGAR BOX GET HERE?

Marvin knew what he was going to shout in her face when she returned. He practiced it once right after the pledge.

"Aha! I **fooooooled** yah!"

Mary Marony turned around. "Fooled who?"

"Nothing," Marvin said, getting to work on his math problems.

Mrs. Bird finally found what she was looking for, the lunch menu. It was under the big blue dictionary on her

16

desk. "Here's what's cooking!" she announced. "Tacos, corn, steamed broccoli,
and vanilla pudding with rainbow
sprinkles. Who would like hot lunch?"

Fourteen people raised their hands.

Marvin leaned back in his chair. He
couldn't wait for his little hide-and-go-
seek game with Miss Scratcho to begin!
Where was Lucy?

"Cold lunch?" Mrs. Bird asked.

Marvin and seven others raised their
hands. Mary Marony raised two hands,
one for Lucy.

Mrs. Bird recorded nine.

Ten minutes later, when the teacher
was reading the picture book *The Story
About Ping* aloud, Marvin looked over
at the doorway.

What was Lucy doing?

At 9:15, when Mrs. Bird finished
the story, Mary Marony walked up to

the teacher and whispered, "Lucy Tinker still isn't back from the bathroom."

Mrs. Bird gasped, "Oh my goodness! I forgot! Please go down and tell her to come up *immediately.*"

A few minutes later when Lucy returned, Mrs. Bird was waiting for her at the door. "Lucy Tinker!" she whispered. "What took you so long?"

Lucy didn't bother whispering back. She just talked in her normal voice. "I couldn't help it. I was constipated."

Mrs. Bird stepped back. "Oh."

Lucy returned to her seat.

As soon as she sat down, Marvin was ready to say it. "Foooo . . . "

And then he saw Lucy pull the pearl-handled comb out of her back pocket. She combed her short, straw-colored hair one more time and then stuffed the comb in her desk.

"Too what?" Lucy snapped.

Marvin's smile changed to a frown. She didn't return the comb to her red bookbag. She didn't discover the misplaced cigar box.

Boo! he thought. I'll have to wait a little longer for the best part of my game.

3

Foooled Yah!

For the next ten minutes, Lucy fiddled with some clay in her desk. She wasn't writing like the rest of the students. Mrs. Bird noticed and came over. She was carrying a book under her arm. "While you were . . . "

The teacher paused. She didn't want to mention the C word. ". . . were busy in the bathroom, we read a wonderful book called *The Story About Ping*. It's about a Chinese duck who was always last in line. I asked the class to write a story about a time they were late for something. Maybe you should read this before you begin writing."

"I like to read," Lucy said, taking the book. "Thank you."

Then she smiled at the teacher.

Mrs. Bird lingered at the new girl's desk. "You have a beautiful smile, Lucy Tinker," she said. "I'm glad you're in my class."

Lucy beamed. "You're the nicest teacher in the whole world," she replied.

Mrs. Bird smiled back and then walked away.

Marvin made a monster face. Boy! he thought. Too bad the teacher didn't know her real name, *Miss Porcupine Scratcho!* She hasn't done a lick of work since she came to class last Thursday. She just fiddles with clay and asks to go to the bathroom whenever there's math problems to do.

Marvin couldn't wait to shout FOOOOOLED YAH! in her face. She'd need a pencil pretty soon. It wouldn't be long now before she would notice that her cigar box was gone!

Marvin looked around at the other students. They were all writing about being late for something. Except for

Audrey. She was madly looking for something in her desk.

"Someone took my pencil!" Audrey blurted out.

The students stopped writing and looked up.

"I got it from my aunt when we went to the circus. It has a clown eraser at the end."

Marvin turned and asked, "Really? What . . . what color was it?"

"It had pink stripes," Audrey replied.

Marvin glared at Lucy Tinker. She *took* it! It was in her cigar box right next to the gold!

"I'm sure it will turn up," Mrs. Bird said. "Everyone keep an eye out. If you see a clown eraser, you know it's Audrey's."

Audrey reached for a plain school

pencil and opened her writing journal.

Marvin noticed Audrey's eyes were getting watery. That pencil was important to her and he knew where it was.

Lucy finally looked in her desk. "Hey, my cigar box is missing."

Marvin decided not to say FOOOOOLED YAH. The timing wasn't right. Instead he just watched Lucy dump things out of her desk.

"It's not here!" she complained.

"Are you missing something, too?" Mrs. Bird asked, throwing her hands in the air.

"Yes! Someone *stole* my cigar box."

Mrs. Bird looked uneasy. "Stole? I don't think we have anyone in our class who is a thief."

Marvin started to get a lump the size of Lucy's clay in his throat. Thief? He was no thief! He was just playing a game of hide-and-go-seek for fun. Lucy was the thief!

"It's not here! My cigar box is gone!" Lucy repeated.

Lucy abruptly turned and whispered to Marvin. "I bet *you* took it to get even with me."

So she finally got the message, Marvin thought. His little game worked.

Mrs. Bird's voice suddenly got an edge to it. "All right, boys and girls. Please take everything out and clean your desks. Maybe Lucy's cigar box accidentally got picked up and placed somewhere else. And maybe the clown pencil will turn up, too."

Everyone started dumping things out of their desks. It got so noisy, Mrs. Bird had to close both doors.

Lucy continued grumbling. "It was not an accident. Someone took my box on purpose. I bet I know who!"

Marvin's temper started to boil. Lucy could take other people's things, but no one could take hers. Well, he would show her!

"FOOOOOOOLED YAH!" he shouted.

Lucy jerked back. Slowly she closed her eyelids, held up her hands,

27

and lunged forward at Marvin.

"Ahhhhh!" Marvin gasped.

He could feel her nails dig into his skin. When he looked down, a few beads of blood popped up on his right hand. He wanted to tell Mrs. Bird, he wanted to push Lucy off her chair, but he didn't do either of those things.

He didn't hit girls, and he didn't tattle. But he did call people names and he wasn't afraid to speak his mind. "Go look in your bookbag, Porcupine Head!" he confessed. "It's there, safe and sound. And when you find it, you should return Audrey's pencil."

Lucy shouted out, "Mrs. Bird!"

Marvin looked at his hand. It was quivering. He got up and got a Kleenex and soaked up the tiny droplets of blood.

Why did I take that dumb box? he thought. Lucy didn't know how to play games. She wasn't any fun. She played for real. *I hate her.*

"Yes, Lucy?" Mrs. Bird said.

"May I check my bookbag in the hall, please?"

Mrs. Bird didn't answer right away. She wasn't sure if she wanted Lucy out of the room again.

Lucy was insistent. "I need to check my bookbag for something. Maybe . . .

I left my cigar box in there." Then she shot a look at Marvin. Mrs. Bird looked relieved. "Yes, please go check. Maybe it *is* there and we can all get on with our day!"

Marvin looked at the mounds of stuff on people's desks. The pearl-handled comb was next to Lucy's stuff on the floor. Audrey was still looking for her special clown pencil.

A minute later, Lucy stood in the doorway holding her bookbag. "My cigar box is not in here!"

Not there? Marvin turned and looked.

Lucy wasn't holding the red book-bag. She was holding an old army bag.

Marvin covered his eyes.

Oh no, he thought.

His game backfired.

He was the one who got fooled!

31

4

The Dirty Truth!

Things got worse.

No sooner had Lucy returned to her desk than Elizabeth squealed, "Hey! That's my pearl-handled comb!"

Elizabeth reached down and picked it up off the floor. A piece of green clay was stuck to the handle.

Mrs. Bird ran her fingers through her bright red hair. "What is going on?"

Marvin slowly uncovered his eyes.

He knew what was going on. He had
put the cigar box in the wrong bookbag!

Elizabeth's!

Lucy Tinker wasn't just a one-time
thief. She was a BIG-TIME THIEF!
She stole Audrey's clown pencil, AND
Elizabeth's pearl-handled comb!

Marvin figured she had probably
stolen the gold rock from a museum.
No doubt it was worth lots of money!

Marvin whipped out his yellow

notebook and made a correction and an addition:

5, 5, ☒ 2, 3

Lucy Porcupine Tinker Stinker had five dumb colors on her five nails, scratched him twice, and stole three things!

Lucy hit her desktop with her fist. "It's not fair."

Marvin laughed. "I agree. It's not fair that you take everyone's stuff."

When Lucy put her head down on her desk and cried, Mrs. Bird came over to comfort her. "I'm sorry about your missing box and I'm sorry about Audrey's pencil. It's so upsetting when this happens. I'm sure they will both turn up. Sometime."

"My comb did," Elizabeth said, trying to be cheerful. "I didn't even know it was missing."

Marvin rolled his eyes.

He felt sick watching the teacher baby Lucy. She didn't deserve any sympathy. Lucy should be sent to the principal, be suspended from school, or thrown in jail!

Marvin looked at the clock. He counted fifty-five minutes until noon.

He couldn't wait! Elizabeth would discover the cigar box in her bookbag when she got her cold lunch. Soon everyone would know that Lucy took Audrey's clown pencil!

In the meantime, he watched a video

with the class on recycling, flipped to a new page in his yellow notebook, and recorded another important number. At least it helped him get his mind off Miss Scratcho, temporarily.

Recycling
500

It took five hundred years for one pair of plastic diapers to decompose in the dirt.

"I wish I had my clown pencil," Audrey moaned.

"I don't even have *one* pencil," Lucy complained.

Marvin stopped jotting down numbers and snarled at Lucy, "That should make you happy. You *never* do any writing."

Lucy held up her hands and bent her fingers like two rainbows, only hers were made out of sharp claws.

Marvin leaned forward and made the meanest face he could. "Scratch me again and I'll . . . "

He decided not to finish his sentence. It seemed more powerful that way. Let her *guess* what he'd do.

Mary Marony interrupted the showdown when she handed Lucy a purple pencil. "I got a package of six of these at the muh-muh-mall last weekend. They were on sale."

"Thank you," Lucy said sweetly, taking the new pencil with a soccer eraser.

"You can keep it," Mary said. "I have four muh-muh-more."

"Better count those, Muh-Muh-Mary," Marvin chimed in. He was sure one of them was already in Lucy's box.

Lucy pointed her yellow fingernail at Marvin. "Don't you know it's mean to make fun of people who stutter?"

Marvin got indignant. "Don't you know it's mean to steal things and to scratch people?"

"I didn't steal anything."

"Sure, sure you didn't!" Marvin held out his hand where his skin was red.

"And I suppose you didn't scratch me either, Tinker *Stinker!*"

"You're MEAN, Marvin!" Lucy shot back.

"You're MEANER!" Marvin replied.

Then he closed his yellow notebook and stuffed it back in his pants pocket.

He didn't mean to make fun of Mary. It was a bad habit he was trying to stop.

Sometimes he just forgot.

Marvin watched the rest of the video about the Hartford landfill, and waited.

At noon, everyone would know who the biggest thief in the world was . . .

Miss Tinker Stinker!

Marvin decided that was the best name for her.

5

The Biggest Thief
in the World

When the lunch bell rang, Marvin raced into the hallway. He couldn't wait to watch the biggest thief in the world get caught!

"Slow down, Mr. Higgins," Mrs. Bird scolded.

Soon everyone was in the hallway lining up. Cold-lunch people were getting their lunches.

"I DON'T BELIEVE IT!" Elizabeth yelled.

Everyone crowded around her,

41

42

including the teacher and Lucy.

"Look what I found in my bookbag! Lucy's cigar box."

Lucy immediately kneeled down and grabbed the box before anyone could open it. She stuffed it inside her bag, then shot Marvin a mean look.

Mrs. Bird sighed, "I'm so glad you found it!"

"I wish someone would find my clown pencil, too," Audrey replied.

Marvin gritted his teeth. The biggest thief in the world just went scot-free!

"What's wrong with your hand?" Elizabeth asked.

Marvin pulled his hand back. "Nothing."

"Mrs. Bird," Elizabeth called. "Marvin should go to the nurse. His hand is all scratched."

"Eeweyee," the class groaned when

43

they saw his pink, puffy skin.

Mrs. Bird hustled over and took one look. "Go to the nurse," she ordered, "right now!"

Marvin pointed to Lucy as he walked by her. "Just you wait," he said.

When Marvin got halfway down the stairs, he realized that he had forgotten his lunch. Oh well, he thought, I can get it after I see the nurse.

Then he got an ear-to-ear grin.

What an opportunity to do something else . . . some real top-secret business!

6

Top-Secret Business

Five minutes later, Marvin hurried back up the stairs. His hand smelled like alcohol and burned a little. When he got to the coat rack outside the room, he saw his bookbag and *hers*.

After he got his lunch, he kneeled down by the army bag. Quickly, he pulled out the cigar box and opened the lid.

There it was next to the gold rock!

The pink pencil with the clown eraser.

Marvin took it, returned the box to the army bag, then tiptoed into the empty classroom. Cuddles made a squeaky noise when he passed by his cage.

Marvin ignored the guinea pig. He had top-secret business to do. He went straight to Audrey's desk and returned her clown pencil.

Yes! he thought.

It felt good to return stolen property.

Wouldn't Lucy be surprised!

Marvin raced out of the room and down to the cafeteria. When he sat down at his class table, Elizabeth was the first to ask how his hand was.

"Fine," Marvin said, biting into a piece of chocolate cake.

"You eat your dessert first?" Lucy
snapped.

Marvin replied with a mouthful
of brown crumbs. "Yup. Surprise
yah?"

Lucy didn't have an answer for him.

Marvin did. "You may have a few
more surprises after lunch, Miss *Tinker
Stinker.*"

Lucy shook her finger at Marvin.

"You shouldn't call people names," she scolded.

Marvin gulped some milk and then burped. "Sorry."

Lucy leaned forward. "I was wrong about you, Marvin Higgins. You're no snake. You're *A PIG!*"

"Ooooooooh, I got *YOUR GOAT* now!" Marvin laughed.

Lucy just stared at Marvin.

And steamed like the broccoli on the hot-lunch plate.

At noon recess, lots of girls were playing jump rope. Lucy was sitting alone in the shade. It looked like she was doing something.

Marvin ran over to bug her again. "I thought you hated to write."

Lucy closed the cloth book and put her soccer pencil down. "You don't know anything about me."

"I know you're mean," Marvin said.

"Funny," Lucy replied. "That's what I know about *you*."

"Where did you get that book from?" Marvin asked. "Someone's desk?"

"MARVIN HIGGINS! One, two, three, four . . . "

"Hey, you can count!" Marvin replied.

"Mr. Adler told me to do that when I get ANGRY! And *you* make me very angry! He also gave me this book when I left my old school."

"Who's Mr. Adler?" Marvin asked.

"None of your beeswax."

Marvin belched again and then ran off to play soccer with the boys.

Shortly after the class returned to the room and sat down at their desks, Audrey made the discovery. "MY CLOWN PENCIL!"

Everyone clapped when she held it up. Marvin knew the timing was perfect.

"FOOOOOLED YAH!" he said to Lucy.

"You better not have taken mine!" Lucy warned.

"All's well that ends well," Marvin hummed. "That's Shakespeare. My grandmother told me that."

Lucy started to count, "One, two, three, four . . . "

Marvin laughed. He knew she was trying to curb her temper.

Ten minutes later, when the class was working on science projects, Audrey checked her bean plants. Suddenly, she yelled, "OH NO! HERE'S MY CLOWN PENCIL!"

Everyone looked up and listened to Audrey's explanation. "I left it here when I was watering the plants this

morning. I remember now, I had just checked off Tuesday."

Mrs. Bird ran her fingers through her bright red hair. "What a crazy day this has been! Everything is turning up where it's not supposed to be!"

Audrey returned to her desk and reached inside. "I don't know where this one came from. Now I have two clown pencils!"

Lucy glared at Marvin while she stepped out into the hall without permission. When she returned, she held her cigar box in her hand. "That clown pencil is mine! It's supposed to be in this box."

Marvin sat up.

Audrey handed it to Lucy. "You went to the circus last month, too? They were handing these clown pencils out for free."

"Yes," Lucy said, starting to sob. "That was the last thing I did . . . with my grandmother."

Mrs. Bird went over and put her arms around Lucy. "Would you like to see Mrs. McCall?" she asked gently. "She's our counselor here at school."

Lucy nodded as she cried. "I miss Mr. Adler. I used to talk to him at my old school."

Mrs. Bird nodded as she wrote a quick note. "Mary, please take this to

the room down the hall. Mrs. McCall is here on Tuesdays."

Mary smiled. "I go to that little room down the hall on Muh-Muh-Mondays when my speech therapist comes. I know where it is."

In a few minutes, Mary returned with Mrs. McCall. She said hello to everyone, smiled, and then took Lucy out for a private chat.

Mrs. Bird sat on Fred's desk and talked to the class. "Boys and girls, Lucy Tinker's mother died a long time ago. Her grandmother helped her father raise her. Three weeks ago, Lucy lost her grandmother to cancer. She and her father moved into her grandmother's empty house, and now she is in our class. Lucy is going to be sad and angry for a while. We need to be understanding."

Marvin looked at the scratches and swallowed hard.

"Lucy told me about her grand-mother," Elizabeth blurted out. "She said she always curled her hair and made her feel pretty. Now it just sticks out all over the place."

When the class started to giggle, Mrs. Bird made a face. "Go on, Elizabeth . . . "

"I felt sorry for her so I said she could borrow my good comb in my red bookbag."

Suddenly, Marvin didn't feel well. He slowly took out his yellow note-book and turned to Lucy's page. He scratched off a few things. But it didn't make him feel any better.

Lucy ~~Porcupine~~ Tinker ~~Stinker~~

5, 5, ~~X~~, 2, ~~X~~

So she didn't steal the pencil or the brush, Marvin thought. She probably didn't steal the gold rock, either.

For the next twenty minutes, the class talked about relatives who had died. Then they quietly took out their math folders and worked on a zoo project.

When Lucy finally returned, she worked with Mary Marony. Marvin had trouble concentrating. He felt a pain, but it wasn't from the scratches on his arm or hand.

It was from the pit in his stomach.

7

Marvin and
the Meanest Girl

Marvin went straight to his room when he got home. He didn't even say hi to his grandmother, who was riding her exercise bike barefoot in the kitchen.

A few minutes later, Nonna knocked on his door. "COME IN," Marvin groaned. He didn't feel like yelling, but his grandmother was hard of hearing. He hoped she would bring a paper tube with her so he could hold it next to her ear. That way he could speak into it with his normal voice and she could still hear him.

Nonna tried to walk between the baseball equipment and game boards. When she stepped on the silver car

from the Monopoly game, she squealed, "*Landsakes!*"

Marvin looked up to see if she was okay, and then rested his head back on the pillow.

Nonna rubbed her foot as she sat down on a baseball glove on his bed. "BAD DAY?"

When Marvin looked at her, she put a paper towel tube next to her ear.

Marvin spoke into it. "She died," he said sadly.

"WHO? CUDDLES?"

"No, Lucy Tinker's grandmother."

"OOOOH, YES. I HEARD ABOUT THAT LAST MONTH. LULU TIN-KER WENT TO OUR CHURCH.

SHE LIVED IN THE YELLOW HOUSE ON THE OTHER SIDE OF THE CREEK."

Marvin continued talking into the tube. "I didn't mean to call her Porcupine Head, or Tinker Stinker. I thought she was the biggest thief in the world. But she wasn't. She wasn't even a little thief. She just missed her grandmother and how she did her hair. I shouldn't have teased her."

Nonna hugged Marvin. "AT LEAST YOU KNOW YOU WERE WRONG. YOU KNOW IT HURTS."

Marvin sat up and put his hand on his stomach. "Yeah, I have a pain here."

Nonna pointed at his hand. "AND A NASTY SCRATCH THERE."

"The nurse put stuff on it," Marvin said. "It'll go away."

Nonna smiled. "I THINK YOU SHOULD ASK THAT LUCY GIRL

OVER SOMETIME TO PLAY
CATCH. YOU HAVE TWO BASE-
BALL GLOVES."

Nonna pulled out the one she was
sitting on.

"Yeah . . . maybe."

"YOU'RE NO ANGEL, BUT
YOU'VE GOT A GOOD HEART,
MARVIN HIGGINS. IF YOU DO
SOMETHING WRONG, YOU AL-
WAYS STRAIGHTEN IT OUT.
BETTER LATE THAN NEVER."

"Yeah," Marvin agreed. Then he
changed the subject. "Any more cake
left, Nonna?"

"PLENTY."

Marvin got up and walked into the
kitchen.

While he was snacking, Nonna looked
out the back window. "LOOKS LIKE
THERE'S A NEW BOY IN THE

NEIGHBORHOOD. HE'S DOWN
AT THE CREEK CATCHING FROGS."

Marvin walked over to the window.
He knew every kid on the block. It was

a new boy, all right. He was wearing a
Yankees cap. The three kids he knew
were Red Sox fans.

"Think I'll go see if he needs any
help," Marvin said. Then he set the
paper tube down on the table and hurried outside.

When he got down to the bank, he
froze.

That wasn't a *new* boy.

It wasn't *even a boy!*

It was Lucy Tinker. She had stuffed
her porcupine hair inside a Yankees
cap. She had a fishnet in her hand. Two
mayonnaise jars filled with creek water
were next to her on the bank.

"Hey, Stink . . . " Marvin bit his tongue.

"Well," Lucy said, looking up.
"If it isn't the burping pig."

Marvin made a face. He looked at
the six rocks that made a perfect path

across the creek and then shook his head. He was not going on *her side*. Instead, he sat down on the cold ground, took out his yellow notebook, and leaned back against a nearby tree. "How many frogs did you catch?" he asked.

"Three. What are you writing down?"

"Something."

"You know, I don't appreciate it when you call me Tinker Stinker."

"Yeah. I have that problem," Marvin replied. "I always give people nicknames. I'm working on it. Sorry, Miss Scratcho. What are you going to do with the frogs you catch?" Marvin asked.

"Eat 'em," Lucy replied.

Marvin sat up! "*You're* going to eat those *baby* frogs?"

"Sure. My dad has a real good recipe for frog legs. You boil them three minutes and then dip them in butter. They're delicious."

When Marvin looked like he was going to get sick, Lucy broke out laughing. "FOOOOOOOOOLED YAH!"

Marvin folded his arms and groaned, "Okay. I guess we're even now."

He watched Lucy pull out a wiggly frog from the creek with her net.

"Hey, I've got a good nickname for you," Marvin said as he pointed his pencil at her. "How about Goosey Lucy?"

"One, two, three . . . " Lucy began counting.

"Tinker Toys?"

"STOP IT, Marvin HIGgins PIGgins!"

Just then, the squirmy frog leaped out of the fishnet and onto the bank.

Marvin jumped up. He hopped over the six stones and crossed the creek. "I'll get him!" he said, cupping his hands.

As soon as he kneeled down on the ground, he trapped the frog and carried him gently over to the mayonnaise jar.

Splash!

The frog landed inside and swam eagerly in the water.

Marvin looked at Lucy.

She wasn't about to say thank you.

"Want to hear the story I wrote?" Marvin asked.

"Maybe."

Marvin took it as a yes as he pulled out his little yellow notebook from his back pocket, inserted another number, and began reading.

5, 5, 2, 3, ^1

"Lucy Tinker has five different colors of fingernail polish on her five nails. She scratched me twice. She's pretty good at catching frogs. She caught three, and I rescued one. Now I need to tell her *one* important thing."

After a short pause, he continued, "I'm real sorry her grandmother died."

Marvin closed his notebook and put it in his back pocket.

There.

He did it.

He tried to straighten things out.

Lucy was quiet for a moment. Then

she handed Marvin her fishing net. "Want to help me catch some frogs?" she asked.

"Sure!" Marvin said. Then he waved the net at Nonna, who was watching from the window.